CHESS

a novella

by Stefan Zweig

illustrations and remarks by Lula Crowder

Copyright © 2024 Decatur Dixon Classics
All rights reserved.
ISBN: 9798875839191

Front cover of the first edition of Stefan Zweig's Schachnovelle released in 1941 with a print run of 300 by the Pigmalion publishing house in Rio de Janeiro, Brazil.

Chess

Zweig on a passenger ship headed to Brazil (1936)

An avid player of the royal game, **Stefan Zweig** (Austrian, born 1881) is best known for novellas (such as *Schachnovelle*, translated here as simply *Chess*, but also *Amok*, and *Burning Secret*), novels (such as our favorite *Beware of Pity*, but also *Confusion* and *The Post Office Girl*), plays, criticism, and biographies. Zweig's work has been both wildly praised and vehemently critiqued. A student of Hippolyte Tains, his writings address themes of emotion, artistry, freedom, pacifism, and rationality in a bid to reveal the psychological and physiological foundations of human nature. Could Zweig's artistic commitment to meta-level humanism been at the root of a lifelong reticence to engage in overt activist politics or does an analysis of his work reflect clear political commitments? Zweig's autobiography, *The World of Yesterday*, was completed in 1942, just before he committed suicide—perhaps the ultimate political act—by barbiturate overdose alongside his second wife, "Lotte" Altmann in Brazil.

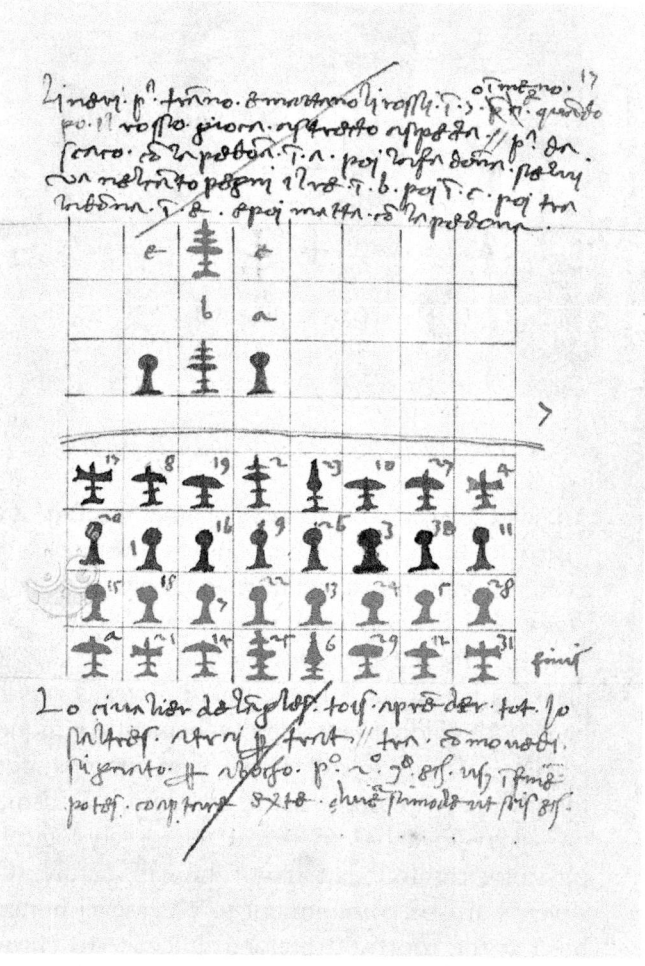

A page from *De ludo scachorum* (On the Game of Chess, or *Schifanoia* (Boredom Dodger)), a Latin manuscript about chess written around 1500 by Luca Pacioli, a leading Renaissance mathematician.

De ludo scachorum was discovered in 2006; some have wondered whether Leonardo da Vinci had a hand in the drawings or perhaps in developing some of the content. Since the mid 1850's, da Vinci's supposed lack of engagement in political affairs in lieu of world citizenship was aligned with an ideology of the artist as an emblem of modernity, as a man without a country. But more recent analyses reveal a more complex situation: his political entailments were robust, and threaded throughout his work. See Rocco, Franco (2013). *Leonardo & Luca Pacioli – the Evidence*. Lex, KY and Versiero, Marco. (2012). "Gift of Liberty and the Ambitious Tyrant: Leonardo da Vinci as a Political Thinker, between Republicanism and Absolutism" in *New Worlds and the Italian Renaissance. Contributions to the History of European Intellectual Culture*. Brill. A page from da Vinci's sketchbooks appears in Zweig's collection.

TO W

The freedom to move around the world, to write, to draw, to think, to address, and even to transcend the iron cage is to find meaning, and ultimately, to be human.

On the large passenger steamship scheduled to depart from New York to Buenos Aires at midnight, the usual hustle and bustle of the final hour prevailed. Guests from the shore mingled to bid farewell to their friends, telegraph boys with tilted hats darted through the crowds, luggage and flowers were dragged around, and children ran wildly up and down the stairs while the orchestra steadfastly played for the deck show.

I stood in conversation on the promenade deck with an acquaintance somewhat away from this commotion when, next to us, flashbulbs erupted two or three times – apparently, some celebrity was being quickly interviewed and photographed by reporters just before our departure. My friend looked over and smiled. "We have an unusual bird on board: Czentovic." I must have looked quite puzzled at receiving this information, so he explained, "Mirko Czentovic, the world chess champion. He has traversed all of America from east to west playing tournament games, and is now heading to Argentina for new triumphs."

Indeed, I now recalled this young world champion and even some details related to his meteoric career. My friend, a more diligent newspaper reader than I, could supplement my recollections with a whole series of anecdotes. About a year ago, Czentovic had suddenly joined the ranks of the most seasoned grandmasters of chess, such as Alekhine, Capablanca, Tartakower, Lasker, Bogoljubow. Since the appearance of the seven-year-old prodigy Rzecewski at the 1922 chess tournament in New York, the intrusion of a completely unknown player into the illustrious guild had never caused such general astonishment. For Czentovic's intellectual qualities did not seem to predict such a dazzling career from the outset. The secret soon leaked out that this chess master, in his private life, was unable to write even a single sentence in any language without spelling mistakes. As one of his annoyed colleagues mockingly remarked, "his lack of education was universally evident in all areas." The son of an impoverished South Slavic Danube boatman, whose tiny boat was run over by a grain steamer one night, the twelve-year-old had been taken in out of pity by the priest of a remote village after his father's death. The good priest earnestly tried to make up through home tutoring for what the taciturn, dull, broad-headed child could not learn in the village school.

But all of his efforts were in vain. Mirko just stared at the characters that had been explained to him a hundred times, always looking at them as if they were alien. His slow-working brain lacked any holding power even for the simplest subjects taught to him. When he had to do calculations, he still had to use his fingers at the age of fourteen, and reading a book or newspaper required especial effort for the already half-grown boy. Yet Mirko could not be described as unwilling or obstinate. He obediently did what he was told, fetched water, split wood, worked in the fields, cleaned the kitchen, and reliably performed every required task, albeit with maddening slowness.

What most annoyed the good priest about the stubborn boy, however, was his total lack of interest. He did nothing without specific instruction, never asked a question, did not play with other boys, and did not seek occupation on his own unless explicitly ordered to do so. As soon as Mirko had completed his household chores, he sat obdurately in the room with a vacant look, like a sheep in the pasture, showing no curiosity whatsoever in the world around him. While the priest, in the evening, smoked his long farmer's pipe and played his usual three games of chess with the police sergeant, the blonde, dull boy sat silently beside them, seemingly drowsy and indifferent, staring at the checkered board from under his heavy lids.

One winter evening, while the two partners were deeply engrossed in their daily game, the bells of a sleigh rang urgently and increasingly closer from the village street. A farmer, his cap dusted with snow, hurried in, stated that his elderly mother was on her deathbed, and begging could the priest please hurry to administer the last rites. Without hesitation, the priest followed him. The police sergeant, who had not yet finished his glass of beer, lit a pipe for his departure and was preparing to put on his heavy boots when he noticed that Mirko's gaze remained unwavering on the chessboard with the ongoing game.

"Well, do you want to finish it?" he joked, fully convinced that the drowsy boy wouldn't understand how to move a single piece correctly on the board. The boy looked up shyly, nodded yes, and took the priest's seat. After fourteen moves, the police sergeant was defeated and had to admit that his loss was not due to any accidental oversight on his part. The second game ended the same way.

"Well, Balaam's ass!" exclaimed the surprised priest upon his return, explaining to the less biblically literate police sergeant that a similar miracle had occurred two thousand years ago when a mute creature suddenly found the language of wisdom. Despite the late hour, the good man couldn't resist challenging his barely literate charge to a game. Mirko easily defeated him as well. He played tenaciously, slowly, and unshakably, without once lifting his broad forehead from the board. But he also played with irrefutable certainty; neither the police sergeant nor the priest could win a game against him in the following days.

The priest, better equipped than anyone to assess his ward's overall backwardness, became increasingly curious about how far this peculiar one-sided talent could withstand a stricter examination. After having Mirko's unruly, straw-blond hair cut at the village barber in an effort to make him appear somewhat more presentable, he took the boy in his sled to the nearby small town, where he knew a corner cafe on the main square with enthusiastic chess players, to whom he himself was not usually much of a match. There was considerable astonishment among the local group when the priest pushed the fifteen-year-old rosy-cheeked boy in his sheepskin fleece and heavy, high clodhoppers into the coffeehouse, where the boy stood

Chess

most bewildered with shy lowered eyes until he was summoned to one of the chess tables. In the first game, Mirko was defeated, as he had never seen the so-called Sicilian Opening with the priest or sergeant. In the second game, he achieved a draw against the best player. From the third and fourth onwards, he handily defeated them all, one after another.[1]

"Well, Balaam's ass!" exclaimed the surprised priest upon his return, explaining to the less biblically literate police sergeant that a similar miracle had occurred two thousand years ago when a mute creature suddenly found the language of wisdom. Despite the late hour, the good man couldn't resist challenging his barely literate charge to a game. Mirko easily defeated him as well. He played tenaciously, slowly, and unshakably, without once lifting his broad forehead from the board. But he also played with irrefutable certainty; neither the police sergeant nor the priest could win a game against him in the following days.

The priest, better equipped than anyone to assess his ward's overall backwardness, became increasingly curious about how far this peculiar one-sided talent could withstand a stricter examination. After having Mirko's unruly, straw-blond hair cut at the village barber in an effort to make him appear somewhat more presentable, he took the boy in his sled to the nearby

---

[1] Why does Zweig make a point of depicting the boy's hair as blonde? This detail appears more than once. Zweig's supposedly ambivalent stance towards the political is troubled by a close reading of works such as *Chess*. If anything, this work represents an address to the racialized Aryan order as re-imagined by the Nazi state.

small town, where he knew a corner cafe on the main square with enthusiastic chess players, to whom he himself was not usually much of a match. There was considerable astonishment among the local group when the priest pushed the fifteen-year-old rosy-cheeked boy in his sheepskin fleece and heavy, high clodhoppers into the coffeehouse, where the boy stood most bewildered with shy lowered eyes until he was summoned to one of the chess tables. In the first game, Mirko was defeated, as he had never seen the so-called Sicilian Opening with the priest or sergeant. In the second game, he achieved a draw against the best player. From the third and fourth onwards, he handily defeated them all, one after another.[2]

Now, exciting events rarely occurred in this small South Slavic provincial town; thus, the surprising appearance of this rural champion immediately became a sensation for the town council. Unanimously, it was decided that the miraculous boy must absolutely stay in the town until the next day so that they could gather the other members of the chess club and, above all, inform old Count Simczic, a chess fanatic, at his castle. The priest, who looked at his ward with an entirely new pride but did not want to miss his obligatory Sunday service despite his joy of discovery, agreed to leave Mirko there alone for further testing.

---

[1] Why does Zweig make a point of depicting the boy's hair as blonde? This detail appears more than once. Zweig's supposedly ambivalent stance towards the political is troubled by a close reading of works such as *Chess*. If anything, this work represents an address to the racialized Aryan order as re-imagined by the Nazi state.

Young Czentovic was accommodated at the expense of the chess club in the hotel and, that evening, saw a flush toilet for the very first time. On the following Sunday afternoon, the chess room was crowded. Mirko, seated for four hours straight in front of the board, defeated one player after another without uttering a single word or even looking up. Finally, a simultaneous game was suggested. It took a while before they could make the uninformed boy understand that in a simultaneous game, he would have to play against several players at once. But once Mirko grasped this concept, he agreed and quickly adapted to the task, slowly moving from table to table in his heavy, creaking shoes, and eventually winning seven out of the eight games.

Now, grand deliberations began. Although this new champion did not strictly belong to the town, local national pride was vividly ignited. Perhaps the small town, whose existence had hardly been noticed by anyone before, could finally earn some recognition and get on the map by sending a famous man out into the world.

An agent named Koller, usually arranging chansonniers and singers for the garrison's cabaret, declared that if they provided funding for a year, he would himself arrange for the young man to be professionally trained in chess by an excellent master in Vienna whom he knew. Count Simczic, who had never encountered such a peculiar opponent in sixty years of daily chess, immediately contributed said amount. From that day on, the astonishing career of the boatman's son began.

Chess

After half a year, Mirko mastered all the secrets of chess technique, albeit with a peculiar limitation that would later be observed and ridiculed in professional circles. Czentovic never managed to play even a single chess game from memory—or as it is technically termed, blindfolded (sans voir). He completely lacked the ability to envision the battlefield purely in the realm of his imagination. He always needed to have the black-and-white square with sixty-four fields and thirty-two pieces physically in front of him. Even during his world fame, he consistently carried a foldable pocket chess set to reconstruct master games or solve problems by visually examining the position.

This seemingly insignificant defect revealed a lack of imaginative power and sparked lively discussions and mockery in the narrow circles. It was akin to a renowned musician or conductor proving incapable of playing or conducting without an open score. However, this peculiar trait did not hinder Mirko's astounding ascent. By the age of seventeen, he had won a dozen chess prizes; at eighteen, he secured the Hungarian championship, and by twenty, he finally conquered the world championship. The most audacious champions, each vastly superior in intellectual abilities, imagination, and boldness, succumbed to his tenacious and cold logic, much like Napoleon succumbed to the ponderous Kutuzov or Hannibal to Fabius Cunctator, of whom Livy reported similarly striking traits of phlegm and imbecility in his childhood.[3]

---

[3] See Erdkamp, P. (1992). Polybius, Livy and the "Fabian Strategy" *Ancient Society*, *23*, 127–147. The Fabian Strategy is one in which frontal assault is avoided in favor of wearing down one's opponent by hit-

Thus, for the first time, an absolute outsider to the intellectual world broke into the illustrious gallery of chess masters. He was a heavy, taciturn peasant lad from whom even the most cunning journalists couldn't extract a single publishable word. Certainly, what Czentovic lacked in polished expressions for the newspapers, he soon compensated for with anecdotes about himself. The moment he stood up from the chessboard, where he was an unrivaled master, Czentovic became a grotesque and almost comical figure. Despite his solemn black suit, pompous tie with a somewhat ostentatious pearl pin, and carefully manicured fingers, he remained the same limited farm boy who swept the priest's room in the village. Awkward and shamelessly clumsy, he sought, to the delight and annoyance of his colleagues, to exploit his talent and fame with petty and often vulgar greed to extract whatever money could be obtained.

He traveled from city to city, always staying in the cheapest hotels, playing in the most pitiable clubs if they granted him his fee. He allowed himself to be depicted in soap advertisements and even sold his name, without caring about the ridicule of his competitors who knew he couldn't write three sentences correctly, for a "Philosophy of Chess" actually written by a small Galician student for the enterprising publisher. Like all tenacious personalities, he lacked any sense of the ridiculous. Since his victory in the world tournament, he considered himself the most important man in the world. The awareness of

---

and-run, guerilla, or indirect means. Fiction and the arts in general, can operate as tactical deployments against the status quo.

having defeated all these clever, intellectual, dazzling speakers and writers in their own field, and above all, the tangible fact of earning more than them, transformed his initial insecurity into a cold and often crudely displayed pride.

"But how could such rapid fame not befuddle such an empty mind?" concluded my friend, who had just shared some classic examples of Czentovic's childish arrogance with me. "How could a twenty-one-year-old peasant from Banat not get a swollen head when he suddenly earns in a week, with a bit of moving around chess pieces on a wooden board, more than his entire village back home does in a year with logging and engaged in the most bitter of toils? And then, isn't it downright easy to consider oneself a great person when one is burdened with not the slightest inkling that a Rembrandt, a Beethoven, a Dante, or a Napoleon ever lived? This lad only knows in his walled-off mind one thing: that he hasn't lost a single chess game for months. Since he doesn't suspect that there are values on our Earth beyond chess and money, he has every reason to be enthralled with himself."

These communications from my friend did not fail to arouse my particular curiosity. Throughout my life, individuals obsessed with a single idea have always intrigued me, for the more one limits oneself, the closer one comes to the infinite; precisely those who seem to be on the fringes of the world construct, in their special matter, a strange and entirely unique abbreviation of the world, much like termites building an unusual and distinctive habitat. So, I made no secret of my intention to scrutinize this peculiar specimen of intellectual singularity more closely during our journey to Rio.

"You will have little luck with that," my friend warned. "As far as I know, no one has succeeded in extracting the slightest bit of psychological material from Czentovic. Behind all of his profound limitations, this cunning farmer hides the great wisdom of not exposing any weaknesses, and he accomplishes this through the simple technique of avoiding any conversation except with fellow countrymen from his own sphere, whom he gathers in small taverns. When he senses an educated person, he retreats into his shell; thus, no one can boast of ever having heard a foolish word from him or measured the supposedly limitless depth of his ignorance."

Indeed, my friend turned out to be right. After three days, I actually began to be annoyed that his tenacious defense technique was more skillful than my determination to get through to him. I had never had the opportunity to personally meet a chess master in my life, and the more I tried to personify such a type, the more unimaginable the mental activity seemed to me—a lifetime revolving exclusively around a space of sixty-four black and white squares. I was well aware, from my own experience, of the mysterious attraction of the royal game, the only one among all games devised by humans that escapes every tyranny of chance and attributes its victories solely to the mind or, rather, to a specific form of intellectual talent.

Chess

But aren't we already guilty of an insulting limitation by calling chess merely a game? Isn't it also a science, an art, hovering between these categories like Mohammed's coffin between heaven and earth, a unique union of all opposing pairs; ancient yet eternally new, mechanical in structure yet effective only through creativity, confined in a geometrically rigid space yet boundless in its combinations, constantly evolving yet sterile, a kind of thought that leads nowhere, a mathematics that calculates nothing, an art without works, an architecture without substance, and nonetheless proven to be more enduring in its existence than all books and works, the only game that belongs to all peoples and all times, and of which no one knows which God brought it to earth to kill boredom, sharpen the senses, and tense the soul.[4]

Where is its beginning, and where is its end? Any child can learn its basic rules, any amateur can try their hand at it, and yet within this unalterably narrow grid, it manages to produce a particular species of masters, incomparable to all others—individuals with a talent uniquely suited to chess, specific geniuses in whom vision, patience, and technique are as precisely distributed as in a mathematician, a poet, a musician, only in a different layering and binding.

---

[4] This passage can be read as a critique of reason. As many scholars of the Frankfurt School attested, the rational promises of the Enlightenment did give us many creature comforts and scientific advances, but also laid the ground for warfare and horrific technological violence. Going further, we might say that rationality and Truth enjoy no necessary congruence.

In times of physiognomic passion, someone like Gall might have dissected the brains of such chess masters to determine whether a particular convolution in the gray mass of the brain, a kind of chess muscle or chess protuberance, was more pronounced in these skulls than in others. And how the case of a Czentovic would have intrigued such a physiognomist, where this specific genius seems infused into an absolute intellectual inertia like a single thread of gold in a hundredweight of dull rock.

In principle, I have always understood the fact that such a unique and ingenious game had to create specific matadors, but how difficult, how impossible it is to imagine the life of a mentally active person to whom the world is reduced solely to the narrow one-way street between black and white. A person who seeks the triumph of their life in a mere back and forth, advancing and retreating thirty-two pieces, a person for whom choosing the knight over the pawn in a new opening already signifies a great feat and their meager corner of immortality in the pages of a chess book – a person, an intellectual, who, without going mad, for ten, twenty, thirty, forty years, repeatedly directs the entire tension of their thinking to the ludicrous goal of cornering a wooden king on a wooden board!

Such a mysterious fool was spatially close to me for the first time, six cabins away on the same ship, and I, the unfortunate one for whom curiosity in intellectual matters always escalates into a kind of passion, should not be able to approach him. I began to devise the most absurd strategies: perhaps tickling his vanity by pretending to conduct a supposed interview for an

Chess

important newspaper or seizing his greed by proposing a lucrative tournament in Scotland. But eventually, I remembered that the most proven technique for hunters to lure a capercaillie is to mimic its mating call; what could be more effective in attracting the attention of a chess master than by playing chess myself?

I have never been a serious chess artist in my own life, for the simple reason that I always engaged in chess casually and exclusively for my pleasure. When I sit in front of the board for an hour, it is by no means to exert myself but, on the contrary, to relieve myself from mental stress. I "play" chess in the truest sense of the word, while the others, the real chess players, play chess "seriously," to introduce a bold new use of the word into the German language. For in chess, as in love, a partner is indispensable, and at that moment, I did not yet know if there were other chess enthusiasts on board besides us. To lure them out of their hiding places, I set up a makeshift board in the smoking room by sitting down with my wife, even though she plays even more weakly than I do.

And indeed, after only six moves, someone passing by stopped, a second requested permission to watch; finally, the desired partner appeared, challenging me to a game. His name was McConnor, a Scottish civil engineer who, as I heard, had amassed a considerable fortune from oil drilling in California. He was a robust man with strong, almost square, hard jawbones, powerful teeth, and a healthy complexion, the pronounced redness of which was probably due, at least in part, to an abundant consumption of whisky. Unfortunately, the noticeably broad, almost athletically vehement shoulders also manifested characteristically in his game, for this Mr. McConnor belonged to that kind of self-possessed successful individuals who perceive even a defeat in the most trivial game as a lowering of their sense of personality.

Accustomed to ruthlessly asserting himself in life and spoiled by factual success, this massive self-made man was so unshakably convinced of his superiority that any resistance seemed to him undue rebellion and almost an insult. When he lost the first game, he became sulky and began to explain ponderously and dictatorially that this could only have happened due to momentary inattention; in the third game, he blamed the noise in the neighboring room for his failure. He was never willing to lose a game without immediately demanding a rematch. Initially, I found this ambitious obsession amusing; eventually, I accepted it only as an inevitable accompaniment to my real intention: to lure the world champion to our table.

On the third day, we succeeded, albeit only halfway. Whether Czentovic observed us from the promenade deck through the ship's window in front of the chessboard or just happened to grace the smoking room with his presence - in either case, as soon as he saw us practicing his art, he involuntarily took a step closer and cast a scrutinizing glance at our board from a measured distance.

McConnor was in the midst of his move. And this single move seemed sufficient to instruct Czentovic on how unworthy of his masterful interest it was to further follow our amateurish efforts. With the same natural gesture with which one of us sets aside a poorly offered detective novel in a bookstore without even leafing through it, he stepped away from our table and left the smoking room. "Weighed and found wanting," I thought to myself, a little annoyed by his cool, contemptuous look.

To express my displeasure in some way, I said to McConnor, "Your move doesn't seem to have impressed the master much."

"Which master?"

I explained to him that the gentleman who had just passed by, casting a disapproving glance at our game, was the chess master Czentovic. Now, I added, the two of us would survive and have to resign ourselves to his illustrious disdain without heartache; poor folks like us just had to make do with what they had.

But to my surprise, my casual disclosure had a completely unexpected effect on McConnor. He became immediately excited, forgot our game, and his ambition began to pound audibly. He had no idea that Czentovic was on board, and Czentovic must absolutely play against him. He had never played against a world champion in his life except once in a simultaneous game with forty others; even that had been terribly exciting, and he had almost won at the time. Did I personally know the chess master? I said no. Did I not want to approach him and invite him to join us? I declined, stating that, to my knowledge, Czentovic was not receptive to new acquaintances.

Besides, what allure could it hold for a world champion to engage with us third-rate players?

Well, I shouldn't have mentioned third-rate players to such an ambitious man like McConnor. He leaned back irritably and bluntly stated that, for his part, he couldn't believe that Czentovic would reject the polite invitation of a gentleman; he would take care of that. At his request, I gave him a brief description of the world champion, and at that, he stormed off, abandoning our chessboard with indifferent disregard, in uncontrolled impatience towards Czentovic on the promenade deck. Once again, I felt that a man with shoulders as broad as his was unstoppable once he had set his will on something.

I waited quite anxiously. After ten minutes, McConnor returned, and not very pleased, it seemed to me.

"Well?" I asked.

"You were right," he replied somewhat annoyed. "Not a very pleasant fellow. I introduced myself, explained who I was. He didn't even shake hands. I tried to tell him how proud and honored we would all be on board if he wanted to play a simultaneous game against us. But he kept his back damn stiff; he was sorry, but he had contractual obligations with his agent that expressly prohibited him from playing without a fee during his entire tour. His minimum is two hundred and fifty dollars per game."

I laughed. "I would never have thought that pushing pieces from black to white could be such a lucrative business. Well, I hope you bid him farewell just as politely."

But McConnor remained dead serious. "The game is scheduled for tomorrow afternoon at three o'clock. Here in the smoking salon. I hope we won't be so easily beaten."

"What? You agreed to the two hundred and fifty dollars?" I exclaimed, quite taken aback.[5]

"Why not? C'est son metier. If I had a toothache, and there happened to be a dentist on board, I wouldn't demand that he pull my tooth for free either. The man is quite right to charge hefty prices; in every profession, the real experts are also the best businessmen. As for me, the clearer a deal, the better. I'd rather pay in cash than have to show gratitude to a Mr. Czentovic and end up thanking him. After all, I've lost more in one evening at our club than two hundred and fifty dollars and didn't even play with a world champion. For 'third-rate' players, it's no shame to be beaten by a Czentovic."

It amused me to notice how deeply I had wounded McConnor's self-esteem with the one innocent term 'third-rate.' But since he was willing to pay for the expensive fun, I had no objection to his misplaced ambition, which would finally introduce me to the acquaintance of my curiosity. We hastily informed the

---

[5] The Munich 1941 chess tournament awarded Gösta Stoltz a trophy and 1,000 Reichsmarks (worth about 400 in 1941, or about $7,300 today). Adjusted for today's rates, $250 in 1941, the original publication date of this novella, would be about $5000.

four or five gentlemen who had declared themselves chess players of the upcoming event and, to be disturbed as little as possible by passersby, not only reserved our table but also the neighboring tables in advance for the impending match.

The next day, our small group gathered at the appointed hour. The middle seat across from the master, of course, was reserved for McConnor, who unloaded his nervousness by lighting one heavy cigar after another and constantly glancing at his watch. But the world champion, as I had already suspected from my friend's stories, kept us waiting for a good ten minutes, which added to the grandiosity of his entrance. He approached the table calmly and composed. Without introducing himself—his impoliteness seemed to convey, "You know who I am, and I don't care who you are"—he began with professional dryness to give the necessary instructions. Since a simultaneous game was impossible due to the lack of available chessboards, he proposed that we all play against him together. After each move, to avoid disturbing our consultations, he would move to another table at the end of the room. Once we made our countermove, since sadly there was no table bell available, we should tap a glass with a spoon. He suggested a maximum move time of ten minutes, unless we wanted a different allocation. Naturally, we agreed to every proposal like timid students. Czentovic assigned himself the black pieces; still standing, he made the first countermove and then immediately turned to the waiting place he had suggested, where he casually leaned and flipped through an illustrated magazine.

It makes little sense to report on the game. It ended, of course, as it had to, with our total defeat by the twenty-fourth move. That a world chess champion easily defeats half a dozen mediocre or submediocre players with his left hand was not surprising. What was rather vexing to all of us was the arrogant manner in which Czentovic made it abundantly clear that he was disposing of us with his left hand. He only cast what seemed like a casual glance at the board each time, looking past us as if we were lifeless wooden figures. This impertinent gesture involuntarily brought to mind the way one might throw a bone to a mangy dog while averting one's gaze. In my opinion, with a bit of sensitivity, he could have pointed out our mistakes or offered encouragement with a kind word. However, even after finishing the game, this inhuman chess automaton uttered not a word.

Instead, after saying "checkmate," he stood motionless in front of the table, waiting to see if we desired another game from him. I had already risen to indicate, through a gesture, that with this paid game completed, at least on my part, the pleasure of our acquaintance was over, helpless as one always remains against thick-skinned rudeness. To my annoyance, McConnor, with a completely hoarse voice, squawked, "Rematch!"

Now McConnor gave more the impression of a boxer gearing up for a fight than of a polite gentleman. Whether it was the unpleasant treatment that Czentovic had subjected us to or just McConnor's pathologically irritable ambition, his demeanor had completely changed. Red-faced up to his forehead, nostrils tensely flared from internal pressure, he visibly perspired, and a sharp crease cut across his clenched lips toward his defiantly jutted chin. I discerned in his eyes that flicker of unbridled passion, akin to what seizes people at the roulette table when, for the sixth or seventh time with ever-doubled stakes, the right color fails to come up.

At that moment, I knew that this fanatically ambitious man would, even if it cost him his entire fortune, continue to play against Czentovic, single or doubled, until he had won at least one game. If Czentovic persisted, he had found in McConnor a gold mine from which he could shovel out a few thousand dollars all the way to Buenos Aires.

Czentovic remained unmoved. "Please," he replied politely. "Gentlemen, you play as Black now."

The second game presented no altered image, except that our circle had grown not only larger but also more animated, with some onlookers becoming curious. McConnor stared at the board as if he intended to magnetize the pieces with his will to win; I sensed from him that he would enthusiastically sacrifice a thousand dollars for the joyous cry of "Checkmate!" against his cold-blooded opponent. Strangely, some of his intense excitement unconsciously transferred to us. Each individual move was discussed with even more passion than before, and we always restrained one another at the last moment before signaling agreement, which brought Czentovic back to our table.
Gradually, we reached the seventeenth move, and to our own surprise, a configuration had emerged that

seemed surprisingly advantageous because we had managed to advance the pawn on the c-file to the penultimate square, c2; all we needed was to move it forward to c1 to obtain a new queen. However, we weren't entirely comfortable with this obvious move; we unanimously suspected that this seemingly hard-won advantage must have been intentionally pushed towards us as bait by Czentovic, who, with his broader perspective, saw the situation much more clearly. But despite our intense collective searching and discussing, we couldn't discern the hidden trap. Finally, just on the brink of the permitted time for deliberation, we decided to make the move.

McConnor had already touched the pawn to move it to the last square when he suddenly felt a firm grip on his arm, and someone whispered urgently, "For God's sake! Don't!"

Involuntarily, we all turned around. A man of about forty-five, whose narrow, sharp face had caught my attention on the deck promenade before due to its strange, almost chalky pallor, must have approached us in the last few minutes while we focused all of our attention on the problem at hand. Hurriedly, sensing our gaze, he added, "If you make a queen now, he'll immediately take it with the bishop on c1. You retreat with the knight. But meanwhile, he moves his pawn to d4, threatening your rook, and even if you check with the knight, you lose and are finished in nine to ten moves. It's almost the same constellation as Alekhine initiated against Bogoljubov in the '22 Pistyan Grand Tournament."

McConnor withdrew his hand from the piece, looking surprised. No less astonished than the rest of us, he stared at the man who had appeared unexpectedly, like an unanticipated angel coming to our aid. Someone capable of calculating a checkmate nine moves ahead had to be a top-notch expert, perhaps even a contender for the championship traveling to the same tournament. His sudden arrival and intervention at such a critical moment felt almost supernatural. McConnor was the first to collect himself.

"What would you advise?" he whispered, visibly excited.

"Move the king away from the threatened line, from g8 to h7. He will probably shift the attack to the other flank. But counter that with rook to c8 to c4; that will cost him two moves, a pawn, and thus the advantage. Then, it's a pawn versus pawn situation, and if you play defensively, you can aim for a draw. That's the best you can achieve."

We marveled once again. The precision, no less than the swiftness of his calculations, was bewildering; it was as if he were reading the moves from a printed book. Nevertheless, the unexpected chance, thanks to his intervention, to draw our game against a world champion had a magical quality. With a nod, we stepped aside to give him a clearer view of the board. McConnor asked once again: "So, move the king from g8 to h7?"
"Yes! Evade above all!"

McConnor obeyed, and we tapped on the glass. Czentovic approached our table with his usual composed step and measured the counter-move with a single glance. Then, on the king's side, he moved the pawn from h2 to h4, just as our unknown helper had predicted.

Excitedly, he whispered: "Move the rook, move the rook, c8 to c4, he must then defend the pawn first. But that won't help him! You capture, without caring about his passed pawn, with the knight c3 to d5, and the balance is restored. Press forward instead of defending!"

We didn't understand what he meant. What he said was Chinese to us. But already under his spell, McConnor moved as directed and without hesitation. Once again, we tapped on the glass to call back Czentovic. For the first time, he did not make a quick decision but looked intently at the board. His brows involuntarily knitted together. Then, he made exactly the move that the stranger had predicted and turned to leave. However, before he stepped back, something new and unexpected happened. Czentovic raised his eyes and scrutinized our ranks; evidently, he wanted to find out who was suddenly putting up such determined resistance.

From this moment on, our excitement grew immeasurably. Until now, we had played without real hope, but the thought of breaking Czentovic's cold arrogance sent a fiery heat through all our pulses.

Chess

However, our new friend had already ordered the next move, and we could—my fingers trembled as I tapped the spoon on the glass—call back Czentovic. And now came our first triumph. Czentovic, who had always played standing, hesitated, hesitated, and finally sat down. He sat down slowly and heavily; but with this, at least physically, the previous from-on-high attitude between him and us was abolished.

We had forced him to descend, at least spatially, to our level. He contemplated for a long time, his eyes immovably fixed on the board, so that one could barely discern the pupils under the black lids, and in deep thought, his mouth gradually opened, giving his round face a somewhat simple appearance. Czentovic studied the board for several minutes more, then made his move and stood up. Instantly, our friend whispered, "A delaying move! Well thought out! But don't engage in it! Force exchanges, absolutely force exchanges, then we can reach a draw, and no God can help him."

McConnor obeyed. In the next moves between the two—we others had long since descended to mere empty spectators—an incomprehensible back and forth began. After about seven moves, Czentovic, after a long pause, looked up and declared, "Draw."

For a moment, total silence prevailed. Suddenly, the waves could be heard crashing, and the radio jazzed from one salon over, every step from the promenade deck was audible, and the faint, fine hiss of the wind rushing through the window gaps could be perceived. None of us breathed; it had come too suddenly, and we all were verily startled by the improbability that this unknown man should have imposed his will on the world champion in a game already half-lost.

McConnor leaned back with a jerk; the withheld breath audibly escaped him in a delighted "Ah!" from his lips. I, in turn, observed Czentovic. Even during the last moves, it had seemed to me as if he had paled. But he knew how to hold himself together quite well. He lingered in a seemingly indifferent stiffness and casually asked, as he calmly removed the pieces from the board, "Do the gentlemen wish for a third game?"

He posed the question purely as a matter of business. But the peculiar thing was that he had not looked at McConnor; instead, he sharply and directly lifted his eye toward our savior. Like a horse recognizing a new, better rider in the saddle, he must have identified his real, his ultimate opponent in the last moves. Involuntarily, we followed his gaze and looked intently at the stranger. However, before the latter could contemplate or even respond, McConnor, in his ambitious excitement, had already triumphantly called out to him: "Of course! But now you must play against him alone! You alone against Czentovic!"

Then something unforeseen happened.

The stranger, who oddly maintained his attentions at the cleared chessboard, started as he felt all eyes upon him and found himself addressed so enthusiastically. His composure faltered.

"By no means, gentlemen," he stammered, visibly flustered. "That is entirely out of the question...I am not even considered...I have not sat in front of a chessboard for twenty, no, twenty-five years...and...and I see only now how impolite I've been by interfering in your game without your permission...Please, forgive my presumption... I certainly do not want to disturb you further." And even before we could collect ourselves from this new surprise, he retreated and left the room.

"But that is completely impossible!" exclaimed the spirited McConnor, pounding his fist. "Totally out of the question that this man hasn't played chess for twenty-five years! He calculated every move, every counterpoint five, six moves ahead. Nobody can do that off the cuff. That's completely out of the question, isn't it?"

With the last question, McConnor involuntarily turned to Czentovic. However, the world champion remained unshakably cool.

"I cannot judge that. Anyway, the gentleman played in a strange and interesting manner; that's why I deliberately gave him a chance," he said, casually rising. In a matter-of-fact manner, he added, "If the gentleman or gentlemen wish for another game tomorrow, I will be available from three o'clock onwards."

We couldn't help but suppress a slight smile. Each of us knew that Czentovic had by no means generously given a chance to our unknown helper, and this remark was nothing more than a naive excuse to mask his own failure. Our desire to see such unyielding arrogance humiliated grew stronger. Suddenly, a wild, ambitious fighting spirit had taken over the peaceful, casual inhabitants of the ship, as the thought of snatching victory from the chess champion in the middle of the ocean—breaking a record that would be flashed around the world by all telegraph offices—fascinated us in the most challenging way. Added to this was the allure of the mysterious, emanating from the unexpected intervention of our savior in the critical moment, and the contrast between his almost timid humility and the unwavering self-confidence of the professional. Who was this stranger? Had chance revealed an undiscovered chess genius? Or was a famous master hiding his name for some unfathomable reason? We discussed all of these possibilities in the most excited manner, and even the most daring hypotheses were not daring enough to reconcile the mysterious shyness and the surprising confession of the stranger with his unmistakable skill. However, we all agreed on one thing: by no means would we miss the spectacle of another match. We decided to do everything in our power to ensure that our helper would play a match against Czentovic the very next day, with McConnor taking responsibility for the material risk.

Since it had been revealed through inquiries with the steward that the unknown man was Austrian, I, being his fellow countryman, was assigned the task of conveying our request to him. It didn't take me long to find the hastily escaped man on the promenade deck.

He lay reading on a deck chair. Before approaching him, I took the opportunity to observe him. The sharply cut head rested in a posture of slight fatigue on the pillow; once again, the strange paleness of the relatively young face, framed by hair that was dazzlingly white at the temples, caught my eye; for some reason, I had the impression that this man must have aged suddenly. As I approached him, he stood up politely and introduced himself with a name that was immediately familiar to me as that of a highly respected old Austrian family. I recalled that a bearer of this name had belonged to the inner circle of Schubert's closest friends and that one of the family members had also been a personal physician to the old emperor.[6]

When I conveyed our request to Dr. B., he was visibly stunned. It turned out that he had no idea that he had just successfully played against a world champion, let alone the currently most successful one. For some reason, this information seemed to make a particular impression on him, as he inquired again and again if I was certain that his opponent had indeed been a recognized world champion. I soon realized that this circumstance made my mission easier and, sensing his sensitivity, thought it advisable not to mention that the

---

[6] Zweig collected autographed musical, literary and historical manuscripts; his heirs continued to develop the collection after his death in 1942 and then donated it to the British Library in 1986. The collection – an astonishing account of European society and Zweig's relationship to it, includes a two-volume printed edition of Schubert's vocal music and weirdly a speech outline by none other than Adolph Hitler. The collection also includes a piano duet by Friedrich Nietzsche. See Searle, Arthur. (1999). *The British Library Stefan Zweig Collection: Catalogue of the Music Manuscripts*. London: British Library.

material risk of a possible loss would be borne by McConnor's own funds. After some hesitation, Dr. B. finally agreed to a match but not without explicitly asking me to warn the other gentlemen not to harbor exaggerated hopes regarding his abilities.

"For," he added with a contemplative smile, "I truly don't know if I'm capable of playing a chess game correctly according to all the rules. Please believe me; it wasn't false modesty when I said that I haven't touched a chess piece since my high school days, more than twenty years ago. And even at that time, I was considered only a player, not one with special talent."

He said this in such a natural manner that I couldn't entertain the slightest doubt about his sincerity. Nevertheless, I couldn't help expressing my surprise at how precisely he could remember every combination of various masters, even if only theoretically. After all, he must have at least engaged in an academic study of chess. Dr. B. smiled again in that strangely dreamlike manner.

I have indeed been engaged with chess, by God, that can be said. But that happened under very special, indeed entirely unique circumstances. It is quite a complicated story, and it could be considered a small contribution to our now more charming era. If you have half an hour of patience..."

He gestured to the deckchair beside him, and I gladly accepted his invitation. We were without neighbors. Dr. B. removed his reading glasses, set them aside, and began: "You were kind enough to mention that you

Chess

recall the name of my family as Viennese. But I suspect you may not have heard of the law firm I managed together with my father and later alone because we handled no cases that were discussed in the newspapers and deliberately avoided new clients as a matter of principle. In reality, we didn't really have a proper law practice anymore but limited ourselves exclusively to legal advice and, above all, to the management of the large monasteries, to which my father, a former representative of the clerical party, was close. In addition, we - today, as the monarchy belongs to history, it's permissible to speak of it - were entrusted with the administration of funds for some members of the imperial family.

These connections to the court and the clergy - my uncle was the personal physician to the emperor, another was an abbot in Seitenstetten - extended back two generations. We merely had to maintain them, and it was a quiet, I would say, almost silent activity assigned to us through this inherited trust. It required little more than strict discretion and reliability, two qualities my late father possessed to the highest degree. He indeed managed to preserve considerable assets for his clients both during the inflation years and those of upheaval through his foresight.

When Hitler came to power in Germany and began his plunder against the possessions of the church and monasteries, negotiations and transactions regarding the preservation of movable assets from confiscation also passed through our hands from beyond the border. We knew more about certain secret political negotiations of the Curia and the imperial house than the public will ever learn. But the very inconspicuousness of our law firm - we didn't even have a sign on the door - as well as the caution of deliberately avoiding all monarchist circles in Vienna ensured the safest protection against unwarranted investigations. In fact, during all these years, no Austrian authority ever suspected that the secret couriers of the imperial house always picked up or delivered their most important mail in our unremarkable office on the fourth floor."

"Now, long before they fortified their armies against the world, the Nazis had begun to organize another equally dangerous and trained army in all neighboring countries—the legion of the disadvantaged, the deprived, the offended. In every office, in every enterprise, their so-called "cells" were entrenched, and at every place, even in to the private rooms of Dollfuß and Schuschnigg, their eavesdroppers and spies sat. Even in our unremarkable law firm, they had, as I unfortunately learned too late, their man. It was, of course, no more than a pitiful and untalented clerk, whom I had hired solely on the recommendation of a priest, to give the outward appearance of a regular operation to the law firm; in reality, we used him for nothing more than innocent errands, let him operate the telephone and organize the files, that is, those files that were completely indifferent and unobjectionable. He was never allowed to open the mail; I wrote all important letters, without leaving copies, personally with a typewriter, took every essential document home myself, and conducted secret discussions exclusively in the priory of the monastery or in my uncle's consulting room. Thanks to these precautions, this eavesdropper saw nothing of the essential events; but by an unfortunate accident, this ambitious and vain fellow must have noticed that he was distrusted and that various noteworthy things were happening behind his back. Perhaps, in my absence, one of the couriers had imprudently mentioned "His Majesty" instead of, as agreed, "Baron Fern," or the scoundrel may have illegally opened letters - in any case, before I could become suspicious, he received orders from Munich or Berlin to monitor us.

Only much later, when I was already in custody, did I remember that his initial carelessness of duty had turned into sudden diligence in recent months, and he had offered almost intrusively several times to take my correspondence to the post. I cannot completely absolve myself of a certain carelessness, but after all, haven't even the greatest diplomats and military leaders been treacherously outplayed by Hitlerism? How exactly and lovingly the Gestapo had already turned its attention to me was then very tangible by the fact that on the same evening that Schuschnigg announced his abdication and a day before Hitler entered Vienna, I had already been arrested by SS men. I had fortunately managed to burn the most important papers, barely having heard Schuschnigg's farewell speech on the radio. The rest of the documents, including crucial evidence for monastery assets that had been deposited abroad and with two archdukes, were hidden in a laundry basket - really at the last minute, before the captors hammered at my door - to be ferried by my old, reliable housekeeper to my uncle."

Chess

Dr. B. paused to light a cigar. In the flickering light, I noticed a slight nervous twitch around the right corner of his mouth, which had caught my attention before and, as I now observed, was repeated every few minutes. It was only a fleeting movement, barely stronger than a breath, but it imparted a strange restlessness to his entire face.

"You probably assume that I will now tell you about the concentration camp, where all those who remained loyal to our old Austria were transferred, about the humiliations, tortures, and torments I endured there. But nothing of the sort happened. I fell into another category. I was not driven like those unfortunates upon whom a long-accumulated resentment was unleashed through physical and mental humiliations. Instead, I was assigned to that other, very small group from which the National Socialists hoped to extract either money or crucial information. In itself, my humble person was of no interest to the Gestapo. However, they must have learned that we, as proxies, administrators, and confidants, had been serving their most bitter opponents. What they hoped to extort from me was incriminating material: material against the monasteries, where they wanted to prove financial malfeasance, material against the imperial family, and material against all those who sacrificially supported the Austrian monarchy.

They suspected - and truly not without reason - that substantial holdings from those funds that passed through our hands were still hidden, inaccessible to their greed. Therefore, they summoned me on the very first day and endeavored to use their proven methods to pry these secrets from me. People of my category, from whom important information or money was to be extracted, were not deported to concentration camps but reserved for special treatment. You may recall that our Chancellor and, on the other hand, Baron Rothschild, from whose relatives they hoped to extract millions, were by no means placed behind barbed wire in a prisoner camp. Instead, they were transferred, seemingly favored, to a hotel, the Hotel Metropole, which also served as the headquarters of the Gestapo, where each captive received a separate room. This 'honor' was also bestowed upon inconspicuous me.

A separate room in a hotel - doesn't that sound quite humane? But believe me, they intended not a more humane but a more refined method for us, the 'celebrities,' not by cramming twenty of us into a freezing barrack but through ostensibly accommodating us in a reasonably heated and separate hotel room. Because the pressure they wanted to apply in extracting the requisite 'material' from us was supposed to work in a subtler way than through brute force or physical torture: through the most sophisticated form of isolation imaginable. They didn't do anything to us - they just placed us in complete nothingness, as nothing on earth creates such pressure on the human soul as nothingness.

By locking each of us individually into a complete vacuum, into a room hermetically sealed from the outside world, that pressure from within, which would eventually burst our lips open, was supposed to be created, instead of from the outside through beatings and cold. At first glance, the room assigned to me did not look uncomfortable at all. It had a door, a bed, a chair, a washbasin, a barred window. But the door remained locked day and night; on the table, no book, newspaper, sheet of paper, or pencil was allowed; the window stared at a firewall; around myself and even on my own body, the perfect nothingness was constructed.

Every object had been taken from me, the watch, so I wouldn't know the time; the pencil, so I couldn't write anything; the knife, so I couldn't open a vein; even the smallest anesthetic like a cigarette was denied to me. I never saw a human face except for the guard who couldn't speak a word and couldn't answer any questions. I never heard a human voice. Eye, ear, no senses received any nourishment from morning till night and from night till morning; one remained hopelessly alone with oneself, with one's own body, and the four or five mute objects: table, bed, window, washbasin. One lived like a diver under the glass bell in the black ocean of this silence and like a diver, even one who already senses that the rope to the outside world has been cut and he will never be pulled back from the silent depth.

There was nothing to do, nothing to hear, nothing to see; everywhere and uninterruptedly, all around you was nothingness, a complete spaceless and timeless emptiness. You walked back and forth, and with you, the thoughts went up and down, up and down, over and over again. But even thoughts, as insubstantial as they seem, need a point of support, or else they begin to rotate and circle senselessly around themselves; they too cannot tolerate nothingness. You waited for something from morning to evening, and it didn't happen. You waited again and again. Nothing happened. You waited, waited, waited, you thought, you thought, you thought until your temples hurt. Nothing happened. You remained alone. Alone. Alone.

That lasted for fourteen days, during which I lived outside of time, outside of the world. If a war had broken out, I wouldn't have known; my world consisted only of table, door, bed, washbasin, chair, window, and wall, and I always stared at the same wallpaper on the same wall; every line of its jagged pattern has etched itself into the innermost fold of my brain, so often I stared at it. Then, finally, the interrogations began. One was suddenly called, not really knowing if it was day or night. One was summoned and led through a few corridors, not knowing where; then one waited somewhere and didn't know where, and suddenly stood in front of a table around which a few uniformed people sat. On the table lay a stack of papers: the files, of which one didn't know what they contained, and then the questions began, the real and the false, the clear and the treacherous, the cover questions and trap questions, and while one answered, strange, evil fingers leafed through the papers, of which one didn't know what they held, and strange, evil fingers wrote something in a protocol, and one didn't know what they were writing.

But the most terrifying thing for me during these interrogations was that I could never calculate what the

Gestapo actually knew about the events in my law firm versus what they wanted to extract from me. As I told you before, I had sent the really incriminating papers to my uncle in the final hour through the housekeeper. But had he received them? Had he not received them? And how much had that clerk betrayed? How many letters had they intercepted, and how much had they already extorted from an unskilled clergyman in the German monasteries we represented? And they asked and asked. What papers had I bought for that monastery, which banks I corresponded with, whether I knew a Mr. So-and-so or not, whether I received letters from Switzerland and or from Steenookkerzeel? And since I could never deduce how much they had already gleaned, every answer became an enormous responsibility. If I admitted to something they didn't know, I might be unnecessarily delivering someone to the executioner. If I denied too much, I harmed myself.

But the interrogation was not the worst part. The worst part was returning after the interrogation to my emptiness, to the same room with the same table, the same bed, the same washbasin, the same wallpaper. Because, once alone with myself, I tried to reconstruct what I should have answered most cleverly and what I should say next time to divert suspicion that I might have brought upon myself with an ill-considered remark. I pondered, I thought through, I searched, I reviewed my own statements, every word I said to the investigating judge. I recapped every question they asked, every answer I gave. I tried to consider what they might have recorded, knowing that I could never find out.

Chess

But once these thoughts were set in motion in the empty space, they didn't stop rotating in my head, over and over again, in ever different combinations, and it went on until I fell asleep.

After every interrogation by the Gestapo, my own thoughts just as relentlessly took on the torment of questioning, probing, and chewing, and perhaps even more cruelly because those interrogations at least ended after an hour, and these never did, thanks to the insidious torture of this solitude.

And always around me only the table, the wardrobe, the bed, the wallpaper, the window, with no distraction, no book, no newspaper, no unfamiliar face, no pencil to jot something down, no matchstick to play with, nothing, nothing, nothing. I soon realized how devilishly meaningful, how psychologically murderous this hotel room system was. In a concentration camp, perhaps one might have had to haul stones until one's hands bled and one's feet froze in their shoes, lying packed together with two dozen people in stench and cold. But one would have seen faces, one would have been able to stare at a field, a cart, a tree, a star, something, anything, while here it was always the same around me, always the same, the horrifying sameness. Here there was nothing to distract me from my thoughts, from my delusions, from my pathological recapitulation. And that was exactly what they intended - I should choke and choke upon my thoughts until they suffocated me, and I couldn't help but to finally spit them out, confessing everything they wanted, ultimately delivering everything that they wanted.

Gradually, I felt how my nerves began to loosen under this terrible pressure of nothingness, and aware of the danger, I strained my nerves to the point of tearing to find or invent some distraction.

To occupy myself, I tried to recite and reconstruct everything I had ever memorized, the national anthem and the nursery rhymes of childhood, the Homer of my grammar school, the paragraphs of the Civil Code. Then I tried to do calculations, adding and dividing arbitrary numbers, but my memory had no gripping power in the void. I couldn't concentrate on anything. The same thought always intervened: What do they know? What did I say yesterday, what do I have to say next time?

This indescribable state lasted for four months. Now - four months, it's easy to write: just ten letters! It's easy to pronounce: four months - two syllables. In a quarter of a second, the lips can quickly articulate such a sound: four months! But no one can describe, measure, or illustrate, not to another, not to oneself, how long a time lasts in spacelessness, in timelessness, and no one can explain how it gnaws and destroys, this nothing and nothing and nothing around you, this always just a table and bed and washbasin and wallpaper, and always the silence, always the same guard who, without looking at you, pushes the food in, always the same thoughts circling in the void, until you go mad. I became aware of small signs that my brain was becoming tangled.

In the beginning, I remained internally clear during the interrogations; I had testified calmly and thoughtfully;

that doublethink, maintaining clarity about I should say and what I should not, was still functioning. But now I could only articulate the simplest sentences, and stutteringly, because, as I spoke, I stared hypnotized at the pen that ran over the paper, as if I wanted to catch up with my own words. I felt my strength diminishing; I felt the moment coming closer and closer when, to save myself, I would blurt out everything I knew, and perhaps more, in which I would betray a dozen people and their secrets to escape the strangulation of this nothingness, and without creating more for myself than a breath of respite. One evening it had really come to that point: when the guard brought me food in this moment of suffocation, I suddenly shouted after him, 'Take me to the interrogation! I want to say everything! I want to confess everything! I will say where the papers are, where the money is! I will say everything, everything!' Fortunately, he didn't hear me. Maybe he didn't want to hear me.

In this extreme crisis, something unexpected happened, offering salvation, at least for a certain period. It was late July, a dark, overcast, rainy day. I remember this detail so precisely because the rain drummed against the windows in the corridor through which I was led to the interrogation. I had to wait in the anteroom of the examining magistrate. One always had to wait during each presentation: even this act of making one wait was part of the technique. First, they shattered your nerves with the call, with the sudden removal from the cell in the middle of the night, and then, when you were already prepared for the interrogation, your mind and will tuned to resist, they made you wait, senselessly and meaningfully wait, one hour, two hours, three hours before the interrogation, to make your body tired, your soul weary. And they made me wait a particularly long time on this Thursday, the 27th of July, standing in the anteroom for two full hours. I remember this date for a specific reason, because in this anteroom, where I - of course, not allowed to sit down - had to stand for two hours with my legs almost giving way, there hung a calendar. I cannot explain to you how, in my hunger for printed words, for something written, I stared and stared at this one number, these few words 'July, 27th' on the wall; I ingested them into my brain. And then I waited again, stared at the door, wondering when it would finally open, and at the same time, I contemplated what the inquisitors might ask me this time, knowing that they would ask me something entirely different than what I had prepared for.

Nevertheless, despite everything, the agony of waiting and standing was also a strange relief, a pleasure, because this room, after all, was a different room than mine, somewhat larger with two windows instead of one, and without the bed and without the washbasin and without the specific crack in the windowsill that I had studied a million times. The door was a different color, a different chair stood against the wall, and on the left, there was a filing cabinet filled with documents and a coat rack with hangers, on which hung three or four wet military coats, the coats of my tormentors. So, I had something new, something else to look at, something different for my starved eyes, and they eagerly clung to every detail. I observed every fold on those coats; for example, I noticed a droplet hanging from one of the wet collars. And as ludicrous as it may sound to you, I waited with absurd excitement to see if that droplet would finally run down the fold or if it would resist gravity and linger longer—yes, I stared and stared breathlessly at that droplet for minutes, as if my life depended on it. Then, when it finally rolled down, I counted the buttons on the coats again, eight on one coat, eight on another, ten on the third; then, I compared the lapels. All these ridiculous, insignificant details touched, played, gripped my famished eyes with a greed that I cannot describe. Suddenly, my gaze became fixed on something. I had discovered that on one of the coats, the side pocket was somewhat puffed up. I approached and believed that I could recognize, from the rectangular shape of the bulge, what this somewhat swollen pocket held: a book! My knees began to tremble; a BOOK!

For four months, I had not held a book in my hands, and the mere idea of a book, in which one could see words queued up, lines, pages, and sheets, a book from which one could read other, new, foreign, distracting thoughts, had something intoxicating about it and yet stupefying. Hypnotized, my eyes stared at the small bulge that formed the book within the pocket; they burned into this one inconspicuous spot, as if wanting to burn a hole in the coat. Finally, I couldn't contain my desire; involuntarily, I pressed closer to the coat. Even the thought of being able to touch a book through the fabric with my hands made my nerves glow to the fingertips. Almost unknowingly, I pressed closer to the coat, staring at the guard the whole time. With my hands hidden behind my back, I touched the book from underneath the pocket, lifting it higher and higher. And then, a grab, a gentle, cautious pull, and

Chess

suddenly, I had the small, not very extensive book in my hands. Only now did I startle at my deed. But I couldn't go back. But where to put it? I slid the volume under my pants behind my back, where the belt held it, and gradually moved it over to the hip so that I could hold it militarily at the seam while walking. Now, the first test was at hand. I stepped away from the coat rack, one step, two steps, three steps. It worked. It was possible to hold the book while walking, as long as I pressed my hand firmly against the belt.

Then came the interrogation. It required more effort on my part than ever because, in reality, I concentrated all my strength, while answering, not on my statement but mainly on holding the book inconspicuously. Fortunately, the interrogation was brief this time, and I managed to bring the book safely to my room. I won't detain you with all the details, as it slipped dangerously from my pants in the middle of the corridor once, and I had to simulate a severe coughing fit to bend down and slide it back safely under the belt. But what a moment when I stepped back into my hell with it, finally alone and yet no longer alone!

Now, you probably assume that I immediately seized the book, looked at it, and read it. Not at all! First, I wanted to savor the pre-pleasure of having a book with me, the artificially delayed and wonderfully exciting pleasure of imagining what kind of book this stolen one would preferably be: very tightly printed, above all, containing many, many letters, many, many thin sheets so that I could read it longer. And then, I wished it to be a work that challenged me intellectually, nothing shallow, nothing light, but something to learn, to memorize, poems, and preferably—what a daring dream!—Goethe or Homer. But in the end, I could no longer contain my greed, my curiosity. Stretched out on the bed in a way that the guard wouldn't catch me if he suddenly opened the door, I tremblingly pulled the volume out from under the belt.

The initial glance was a disappointment and even a kind of bitter anger: this book, acquired with such tremendous danger, with such glowing anticipation, turned out to be nothing more than a chess manual, a collection of a hundred and fifty master games. If I hadn't been locked up, closed off, I would have, in a fit of rage, hurled the book through an open window, for what could, what should I do with this nonsense? As a boy in high school, like most others, I had occasionally tried my hand at a chessboard out of boredom.

But what use was this theoretical stuff to me? You can't play chess without a partner, and certainly not without pieces, without a board. Annoyed, I flipped through the pages, hoping to find something readable, an introduction, instructions; but all I found were the bare square diagrams of individual master games and, beneath them, initially incomprehensible symbols like a1-a2, Qf1 - g3, and so on. It all seemed like a kind of algebra for which I had no key.

Gradually, I deciphered that the letters a, b, c stood for the ranks, the numbers 1 to 8 for the files, determining the respective position of each piece; thus, the purely graphic diagrams were given a language. Perhaps, I thought, I could construct a kind of chessboard in my cell and then try to replay these games; it seemed like a

Chess

heavenly sign that my sheet happened to be roughly checkered. Properly folded, it could eventually be arranged to form sixty-four squares. So, I initially hid the book under the mattress and ripped out only the first page. Then, using small crumbs saved from my bread, I began, in a crude and imperfect manner, to mold the chess pieces—king, queen, and so on; after endless effort, I could finally attempt to reconstruct the position from the chess book on the checkered sheet.

However, when I tried to replay the entire game, it initially failed completely with my ludicrous crumb pieces, of which I had darkened half with dust for distinction.

In the first few days, I constantly confused myself; five times, ten times, twenty times, I had to start this one game over from the beginning. But who on earth had as much unused and useless time as I, the slave of nothing, who had so much boundless greed and patience at his disposal? After six days, I already played the game flawlessly to the end, after another eight days, I no longer needed the crumbs on the sheet to visualize the position from the chess book, and after another eight days, even the checkered sheet became unnecessary; the initially abstract symbols of the book, a1, a2, c7, c8, were automatically transformed into visual, plastic positions behind my forehead. The transition was complete: I had projected the chessboard with its pieces inward, and thanks to the mere formulas, I surveyed the respective position, just as a skilled musician needs only the sight of the score to hear all the voices and their harmony.

After another fourteen days, I was effortlessly able to replay every game from the book by heart—or, as the technical term goes, blindfolded; only now did I begin to understand what an immense benefit my audacious theft had gained for me. Because all at once, I had an activity—a senseless, purposeless one, if you will, but still one that obliterated the nothingness around me. With the hundred and fifty tournament games, I possessed a wonderful weapon against the oppressive monotony of space and time. To keep the thrill of the new occupation unbroken, I allotted myself a rule for every day: two games in the morning, two games in the afternoon, and a quick repetition in the evening. With that, my day, which otherwise stretched formlessly like gelatin, was filled; I was occupied without tiring myself, for chess has the wonderful advantage that, by concentrating mental energy on a narrowly defined field, it does not relax the brain, even with the most demanding mental effort, but rather sharpens its agility and resilience.

Gradually, an artistic, joyful understanding began to awaken in me as I mechanically replayed the master games. I learned to understand the subtleties, tricks, and sharpness in attack and defense; I grasped the technique of anticipating, combining, riposting, and soon recognized the personal touch of each chess master in their individual play as unerringly as one detects a poet's verses from just a few lines; what had begun as merely a time-filling occupation became enjoyment, and the figures of the great chess strategists, such as Alekhine, Lasker, Bogoljubow, Tartakower, became beloved companions in my solitude. Endless variety animated the silent cell every day, and precisely the regularity of my exercises restored the shaken certainty to my thinking ability: I felt my brain refreshed and, through constant mental discipline, even somewhat newly sharpened.

That I thought more clearly and concisely became increasingly apparent, especially during the interrogations; unconsciously, I had perfected my defense against false threats and concealed moves on the chessboard; from that moment on, I never showed vulnerability during interrogations, and it even seemed to me that the Gestapo agents were gradually beginning to regard me with a certain respect. Perhaps, in silence, as they saw everyone else collapse, they wondered from which secret sources I drew the strength for such unwavering resistance.

This period of happiness, during which I systematically replayed the hundred and fifty games of that book day after day, lasted about two and a half to three months. Then, unexpectedly, I hit a dead end. Suddenly, I found myself once again facing nothingness. As soon as I had played each individual game twenty or thirty times, it lost the appeal of novelty, surprise. The previously exciting and stimulating power was exhausted. What sense was there in repeating games over and over when I knew every move by heart? As soon as I made the first move, the sequence of moves played out automatically in me. There was no more surprise, no tension, no problems. To occupy myself, to create the necessary effort and distraction that had become indispensable, I actually needed a different book with different games. Since this was completely impossible, there was only one way to proceed: I had to invent new games instead of the old ones. I had to try to play with myself or, rather, against myself.

I don't know to what extent you have contemplated the mental situation in this game of games. However, even the most cursory consideration should be sufficient to clarify that in chess, as a purely intellectual game detached from chance, it becomes a logical absurdity to want to play against oneself. The fundamental attractiveness of chess lies in the fact that its strategy develops differently in two different minds, and that in this intellectual warfare, Black is unaware of White's specific maneuvers and constantly tries to guess and thwart them, while at the same time, White seeks to surpass and counteract the secret intentions of Black. If Black and White were one and the same person, the nonsensical situation would arise that one and the same mind should simultaneously know and not know something, that, functioning as White's partner, it could completely forget on command what it wanted and intended as Black's partner just a minute before. Such doublethink actually requires a complete split of consciousness, an arbitrary ability to switch on and off mental functions like a mechanical apparatus; wanting to play against oneself in chess, therefore, entails a paradox as absurd as trying to jump over one's own shadow.

Well, to cut a long story short, I attempted this impossibility, this absurdity in my desperation. But I had no choice but to embrace this nonsense to avoid succumbing to sheer madness or complete mental decay. I was forced by my terrible situation to at least attempt this division into a Self-Black and a Self-White, to prevent being overwhelmed by the horrendous nothingness around me."

Dr. B. leaned back in his reclining chair and closed his eyes for a minute. It was as if he wanted to forcibly suppress a disturbing memory. Again, the strange twitch he couldn't control now occurred around the left corner of his mouth. Then he raised himself a bit higher in his armchair.

"So - up to this point, I hope I have explained everything to you quite clearly. But unfortunately, I'm by no means sure whether I can illustrate the further details to you in a similar manner. Because this new activity required such an unconditional tension of the brain that it made any simultaneous self-control impossible. I already hinted that, in my opinion, it's nonsense in itself to want to play chess against oneself; but even this absurdity would still have a minimal chance with a real chessboard in front of you, because the chessboard, by its reality, still allows for a certain distance, a material externalization. In front of a real chessboard with real pieces, you can at least take breaks in contemplation, you can physically position yourself on one side of the table or the other and thus consider the situation from the standpoint of Black and then from the standpoint of White. But compelled, as I was, to project these battles against myself, or, if you will, within myself, into an imaginary space, I was forced to hold the respective positions on the sixty-four squares clearly in my mind.

Additionally, I had to calculate not only the current configuration but also the possible future moves of both partners, and - I know how absurd all this sounds - to imagine them for myself twice and thrice, no, sixfold, eightfold, twelvefold, four or five moves ahead for each of my selves, for Black and White. I must ask you to endure this madness - in this game in the abstract realm of imagination, as White, I had to calculate four or five moves ahead and similarly as Black, anticipating all the situations that would arise in the development, in a sense, precomputing them with two brains, with the White brain and the Black brain. But even this dual self was not the most dangerous part of my absurd experiment, but that I suddenly lost the ground under my feet and fell into the bottomless void by inventing games on my own.

The mere replaying of the master games, as I had practiced in the preceding weeks, had ultimately been nothing but a reproductive performance, a pure recapitulation of given material, and as such, not more strenuous than if I had memorized poems or legal paragraphs. It was a limited, disciplined activity and therefore an excellent mental exercise.

The two games I practiced in the morning plus the two in the afternoon represented a specific task that I completed without any excitement; they replaced a normal occupation for me, and besides, if I erred in the course of a game or didn't know what to do next, the book still provided a guide. Only for this reason, this activity had been so beneficial and rather soothing for my shaken nerves because replaying other people's games didn't involve me directly; whether Black or White won was a matter of indifference to me, it was still Alekhine or Bogoljubow fighting for the champion's laurels, and my own person, my mind, my soul enjoyed merely as a spectator, as a connoisseur, the vicissitudes and beauties of those games.

But from the moment I tried to play against myself, I began unconsciously to challenge myself. Each of my two selves, my Black self and my White self, had to compete against each other and each, in turn, became ambitious, impatient, hungry to win; I eagerly awaited each move as Black, wondering what White would do next. Each of my two selves triumphed when the other made a mistake and simultaneously got annoyed at its own clumsiness.

All of this seems senseless, and indeed, such artificial schizophrenia, such a split in consciousness with its infusion of dangerous excitement, would be unthinkable for a normal person in a normal state. But do not forget that I was violently torn from all normality, a prisoner, innocently confined, tortured for months with refined loneliness, a person who longed to discharge his accumulated rage against something. And since I had nothing else but this nonsensical game against myself, my anger, my desire for revenge, fanatically merged into this game. Something in me wanted to be right, and I only had this other self in me that I could fight; so, during the game, I worked myself into an almost manic frenzy. In the beginning, I thought calmly and deliberated; I inserted breaks between one and the other game to recover from the strain. But gradually, my irritated nerves no longer allowed me to wait. As soon as my White self made a move, my Black self was already feverishly anticipating; as soon as one game ended, I challenged myself to the

Chess

next, for each time one of the two chess-selves was defeated and demanded a rematch. I will never be able to even remotely express how many games I played against myself amidst this insane insatiability during these last months in my cell—perhaps a thousand, perhaps more. It was an obsession I couldn't resist; from morning until night, I thought of nothing but bishops and pawns and rooks and kings and a and b and c and checkmate and castling; with my entire being and feeling, it thrust me into the checkered square.

What started as the joy of playing became a passion, and then from passion, a compulsion, a mania, a frenetic fury that not only permeated my waking hours but gradually invaded my sleep. I could only think of chess, chess movements, chess problems; sometimes I woke up with a damp forehead and realized that I must have unconsciously continued to play in my sleep. And when I dreamed of people, it happened exclusively in the movements of the bishop, the rook, in the back and forth of the knight's jump.

Even when I was summoned for interrogation, I could no longer think concisely about my responsibility; I have the sensation that during these last interrogations, I must have expressed myself rather confusedly because the interrogators sometimes looked at each other strangely. But in reality, I eagerly waited, while they asked and deliberated, in my wretched greed, only to be returned to my cell to continue my game, my mad game, a new game and another and another. Every interruption became a disturbance to me; even the quarter-hour when the guard tidied up the prison cell, the two minutes when he brought me food, tortured my feverish impatience; sometimes, the bowl with the meal remained untouched in the evening; I had forgotten to eat above my play.

How this dreadful, indescribable condition led to a crisis, I cannot myself report. All I know is that one morning I woke up, and it was a different awakening than usual. My body seemed detached from me; I rested soft and pleasant. A dense, good fatigue, as I hadn't known for months, lay on my eyelids, so warm and benevolent that at first, I couldn't make myself open my eyes. For minutes, I lay awake, enjoying this heavy dullness, warm with pleasantly numbed senses. Suddenly, it seemed to me as if I heard voices behind me, living human voices, softly whispering voices speaking words, and you can't imagine my delight, for I hadn't heard other words for months, almost a year, than the harsh, sharp, and evil ones from my persecutors. 'You're dreaming,' I told myself. 'You're dreaming! Do not open your eyes under any circumstances! Let this dream last, or else you'll see the cursed cell around you, the chair, the washbasin, and the table, and the wallpaper with the eternally same pattern. You're dreaming - keep dreaming!'

But curiosity prevailed. I slowly and cautiously opened my eyelids. And wonder: I found myself in a different room, a broader, and more spacious than my hotel cell. An unbarred window let in free light and offered a view of trees, green trees swaying in the wind instead of my rigid firewall; the walls were white and smooth, the ceiling white and high above me - indeed, I lay in a new, unfamiliar bed, and truly, it was no dream; behind me, human voices were softly whispering. Involuntarily, I must have moved vehemently in my surprise because I heard an approaching step. A woman came toward me with soft footfalls, a woman with a white cap over her hair, a caregiver, a nurse. A shiver of delight fell upon me: I hadn't seen a woman in a year. I stared at the charming figure, and it must have been a wild ecstatic gaze because she urgently reassured me, 'Calm down! Stay calm!' But I listened to her voice - was this not a human speaking? Was there really still a person on Earth who did not torture or torment me? And moreover - an incredible miracle! — a soft, warm, almost tender woman's voice. I greedily stared at her mouth because in this hellish year, it had become unimaginable to me that one person could speak to another. She smiled at me - yes, she smiled, there were still people who could kindly smile — then she placed her finger admonishingly on her lips and walked away quietly. But I could not obey her command. I had not yet had my fill of the miracle. Violently, I tried to sit up in the bed to look after her, to look after this miracle of a human being who was kind.

But as I tried to sit up on the edge of the bed, I couldn't. Where my right hand, fingers, and joints had been, I felt something strange, a thick, large white bundle, an extensive bandage. I stared at this white, thick, foreign thing on my hand first in confusion, then I began to slowly understand where I was and to consider what might have happened to me. I must have been wounded, or I had injured my hand myself. I was in a hospital.

At noon, the doctor arrived, a friendly elderly gentleman. He knew my family name and mentioned my uncle, the imperial physician, so respectfully that I immediately felt he meant well with me. In the course of our conversation, he asked various questions, especially one that surprised me - whether I was a mathematician or chemist. I denied it. 'Strange,' he murmured. 'In your fever, you kept shouting strange formulas - C3, C4. None of us understood.' I inquired about what had happened to me. He smiled strangely. 'Nothing serious. An acute irritation of the nerves,' and added, after glancing around cautiously, quietly, 'Finally, quite understandable. Since March 13th, isn't it?' I nodded. 'No wonder with this method,' he muttered. 'You're not the first. But don't worry.' From the way he reassuringly whispered this to me, and with comfort in his gaze, I knew that I was in good hands with him.

Two days later, the kind doctor explained quite openly to me what had happened. The guard had heard me screaming loudly in my cell and initially thought that someone had entered, and I was arguing with them. However, as soon as he showed himself at the door, I had lunged at him, shouting wild phrases like, 'Draw your weapon, you scoundrel, you coward!' I had tried to grab him by the throat and attacked him so fiercely that he had to call for help. When they dragged me in my frenzied state for a medical examination, I broke free, rushed to the window in the corridor, smashed the glass, and in the process, cut my hand - you can still see the deep scar here. I had spent the first few nights in the hospital in a kind of brain fever, but now, he found my sensorium entirely clear. 'Of course,' he added softly, 'I better not report this to the authorities, or they might take you back there again. Trust me, I will do my best.'

What this helpful doctor reported to my tormentors about me is beyond my knowledge. In any case, he achieved what he wanted: my release. Perhaps he declared me mentally unfit, or maybe I had become unimportant to the Gestapo, because in the meantime Hitler had occupied Bohemia, and thus, the case of Austria was settled for him.

So, all I had to do was sign a commitment to leave our homeland within fourteen days, and these fourteen days were so filled with the thousand formalities that a former world citizen needs for emigration nowadays - military papers, police, taxes, passport, visa, health certificate - that I had no time to dwell on the past. Apparently, mysterious regulating forces operate in our brains, automatically shutting off what can become burdensome and dangerous to the soul because every time I wanted to reflect upon my time in the cell, the light in my brain, so to speak, went out; only after weeks and weeks, actually only here on the ship, did I find the courage to recall what had happened to me.

And now you will understand why I behaved so terribly and probably incomprehensibly to your friends. I was just strolling casually through the smoking lounge when I saw your friends sitting in front of the chessboard; involuntarily, I felt my foot rooted in astonishment and terror. Because I had completely forgotten that one can play chess on a real chessboard with real pieces, forgotten that in this game, two completely different people are sitting face to face. It truly took me a few minutes to remember that what those players were doing there was essentially the same game that I had attempted in my helplessness for months against myself. The ciphers I used during my grim exercises had only been substitutes and symbols for these bony figures; my surprise that this piece-moving on the board was the same as my imaginary fantasizing in mental space might have been similar to that of an astronomer who, using the most complicated methods on paper, calculates a new planet and then actually sees it in the sky as a white, material, substantial star. Staring at the board as if held by a magnetic force, I saw my schemes, knight, rook, king, queen, and pawns as real, carved wooden figures; to survey the position of the game, I involuntarily had to transform them back from my abstract numerical world into that of the moving pieces. Gradually, curiosity overcame me to observe a real game between two partners. And then the embarrassing happened: I, forgetting all politeness, intervened in your game. But this wrong move by your friend hit me like a stab in the heart. It was a pure instinctual act that I held him back, an impulsive grasp, like one instinctively seizes a child leaning over a railing without thinking. Only later did I realize the gross rudeness of which I had made myself guilty by my intrusion."

I hurried to assure Dr. B. how delighted we all were to owe this encounter to chance and that, after everything he had confided in me, it would be doubly interesting for me to watch him tomorrow during the impromptu tournament. Dr. B. made a restless movement. "No, don't expect too much. It's just supposed to be a test for me... a test to see if I... if I'm even capable of playing a normal chess game, a game on a real chessboard with actual pieces and a living partner... because now I'm increasingly doubting whether those hundreds and maybe thousands of games I played were indeed proper chess games and not just a kind of dream chess, a feverish chess, a fever game where, as always in dreams, intermediate stages were skipped. Surely you're not seriously expecting me to presume to challenge a chess master, let alone the world's first. What interests and intrigues me is solely the posthumous curiosity to determine whether the chess I played in the cell was still chess or was it madness, whether I was still just before or already beyond the dangerous precipice back then - only this, only this alone."

At that moment, the ship's gong calling us to dinner sounded from the end of the ship. Dr. B. had told me everything in much more detail than I am summarizing here - we must have chatted for almost two hours. I thanked him warmly and bid him farewell. But I had not yet made it to the deck when he came after me, visibly nervous and even somewhat stuttering: "One more thing! Would you be so kind as to inform the gentlemen in advance, so that I don't appear rude afterwards: I am only playing a single game... It is meant to be nothing more than the final stroke under an old account - a definitive settlement and not a new beginning... I don't want to fall into that passionate gaming fever a second time, which I can only look back upon with horror... and by the way... the doctor warned me back then as well... expressly warned me. Anyone who has succumbed to a mania remains forever at risk, and even if healed, with chess poisoning, one better not get close to any chessboard... So you understand: only this one trial game for myself and nothing more."

Punctually at the agreed-upon hour, three o'clock, we gathered the next day in the smoking salon. Our group had expanded by two enthusiasts of the royal game, two ship officers who had requested leave from duty just to watch the tournament. Czentovic also did not keep us waiting, and after the obligatory color selection, the memorable game between this *Homo obscurissimus* and the famous world champion began. I regret that it was played only for us, entirely incompetent spectators, and its course is as lost to the annals of chess as Beethoven's piano improvisations are to music. Although we tried to reconstruct the game from memory in the following afternoons, it was in vain; most likely, we all focused too passionately on the two players rather than on the progress of the game.

The intellectual contrast in the habits of the two partners became increasingly tangible during the game. Czentovic, the veteran, remained immobile like a block throughout, his eyes strict and fixed on the chessboard; thinking seemed to be a downright physical effort for him, forcing all his organs to the utmost concentration. Dr. B., on the other hand, moved completely casually and unburdened. As the true amateur in the most positive sense of the word who plays only for the pleasure of the game, a 'diletto', he kept his body completely relaxed. During the first pauses, he chatted with us, lighting a cigarette with a light touch, and only glanced directly at the board for a minute when it was

Chess

his turn. Each time, it seemed as though he had anticipated the opponent's move in advance.

The obligatory opening moves occurred quite rapidly. It was only around the seventh or eighth move that something like a specific plan seemed to develop. Czentovic extended his contemplative pauses; we sensed that the real struggle for dominance was beginning. But to be fair, the gradual development of the situation, like any true tournament game for us laymen, was quite disappointing. The more the pieces intertwined into a peculiar configuration, the more impenetrable the actual state became for us. We couldn't perceive what either opponent intended or who was actually in the advantageous position. We could only see that individual pieces advanced like levers to break through the enemy front, but we couldn't grasp the strategic intention in this to-and-fro, as with these superior players, every move was always calculated several moves ahead. Gradually, a paralyzing fatigue set in, mainly caused by Czentovic's endless contemplative pauses, which also visibly irritated our friend.

I observed with concern how, as the game dragged on, he began to fidget more and more restlessly in his chair, lighting one cigarette after another out of nervousness, occasionally reaching for a pencil to jot something down. Then he would order a mineral water, which he hastily downed, glass after glass; it was obvious that he was calculating a hundred times faster than Czentovic. Every time the latter, after prolonged deliberation, decided to move a piece forward with his heavy hand, our friend would smile as someone who sees something long-awaited finally happening and would immediately counter. He must have calculated all the opponent's possibilities with his rapid-working mind in his head; the longer, therefore, Czentovic's decision was delayed, the more his impatience grew, and an annoyed and almost hostile expression formed around his lips during the wait.

But Czentovic was not to be rushed. He considered his moves stubbornly and silently, pausing longer and longer as the field of pieces became more exposed. At the forty-second move, after a grueling two and three-quarter hours, we were all tired and almost indifferent around the tournament table. One of the ship officers had left, another had taken out a book for reading and only glanced up for a moment with each change. But then, suddenly, the unexpected happened with one of Czentovic's moves. As soon as Dr. B. noticed that Czentovic was grasping the knight to move it forward, he crouched down like a cat ready to pounce. His whole body began to tremble, and as soon as Czentovic made the knight move, he sharply pushed the queen forward, said triumphantly, "There! Done!" leaned back, crossed his arms over his chest, and looked challengingly at Czentovic. A hot light suddenly glowed in his pupil.

Unconsciously, we leaned over the board to understand the move so triumphantly announced. At first glance, no direct threat was visible. Our friend's statement must refer to a development that we short-sighted dabblers could not yet calculate. Czentovic was the only one among us who had not moved at that challenging announcement; he sat as immovable as if

Chess

he had completely ignored the insulting "Done!" Nothing happened. You could hear, as we all involuntarily held our breath, the ticking of the clock placed on the table to determine the move time. Three minutes passed, seven minutes, eight minutes - Czentovic did not move, but it seemed to me as if, from an inner effort, his thick nostrils expanded even wider. Our friend found this silent waiting just as unbearable as we did. With a jerk, he suddenly stood up and began to pace back and forth in the smoking room, first slowly, then faster and faster.

We all looked at him somewhat surprised, but none more alarmed than I, for I noticed that despite all the violence of this up and down, his steps always measured the same span of space; it was as if he encountered an invisible barrier in the middle of the empty room each time, forcing him to turn around.
And shuddering, I realized that this unconscious pacing reproduced the dimensions of his former cell; this is exactly how he must have paced up and down like a caged animal in the months of confinement, hands clenched and shoulders hunched; he must have walked up and down a thousand times there, the red lights of madness fixed in a feverish gaze. But his reasoning still seemed completely intact, for from time to time, he impatiently turned to the table to see if Czentovic had decided. But nine minutes passed, ten minutes. Then finally, what none of us had expected happened. Czentovic slowly lifted his heavy hand, which had been motionless on the table until then.

We all looked eagerly at his decision. But Czentovic made no move; instead, the back of his upturned hand pushed all the pieces slowly off the board with a decisive jerk. Only the next moment did we understand: Czentovic had resigned. He had capitulated to avoid being visibly checkmated in front of us. The improbable had happened; the world champion, the champion of countless tournaments, had surrendered to an unknown, a man who had not touched a chessboard in twenty or twenty-five years. Our friend, the anonymous, the ignotus, had defeated the best chess player in the world in open combat! Unconsciously, we had all risen in our excitement, one after another. Each of us felt the need to say or do something to vent our joyful shock. The only one who remained immobile in his calm was Czentovic. Only after a measured pause did he lift his head and gaze at our friend with a stony look. "Another game?" he asked.

"Of course," replied Dr. B. with an enthusiasm that made me uncomfortable, and before I could remind him of his resolution to stop after one game, he immediately sat down again and began to set up the pieces with feverish haste. He arranged them with such intensity that a pawn slipped through his trembling fingers to the floor twice; my already uncomfortable unease in the face of his unnatural excitement grew into a kind of fear. A visible excitement had come over the previously quiet and calm man; the twitching around his mouth became more frequent, and his body trembled as if shaken by a sudden fever.

"Not now!" I whispered to him softly. "Not now! Let it be enough for today! It's too exhausting for you."

"Exhausting? Ha!" he laughed loudly and maliciously. "I could have played seventeen games meanwhile instead of this dawdling! Exhausting is only not falling asleep at this pace! - Well! Start already! Now!"

He said these last words in a vehement, almost rough tone to Czentovic. The latter looked at him calmly and deliberately, but his stonily fixed gaze had the air of a clenched fist. Suddenly something new stood between the two players; a dangerous tension, a passionate hatred. They were no longer two partners trying out their skills playfully; they were two enemies sworn to destroy each other. Czentovic hesitated for a long time before making the first move, and I had the distinct feeling that he hesitated on purpose. Apparently, the trained tactician had already figured out that his slowness was tiring and irritating the opponent. He took no less than four minutes before making the most normal, simplest of all openings by moving the king's pawn two squares as usual. Immediately, our friend moved his king's pawn to meet him, but again Czentovic made an endless, almost unbearable pause; it was as if a strong lightning struck and one waited with pounding heart for the thunder, and the thunder didn't come. Czentovic did not move. He pondered quietly, slowly, and, as I felt more and more certain, maliciously slowly; but this gave me ample time to observe Dr. B. He had just downed the third glass of water; I involuntarily remembered him talking about his feverish thirst in the cell. All symptoms of abnormal excitement were clearly evident; I saw his forehead becoming moist, and the scar on his hand redder and sharper than before. But he held himself together.

Only when, during the fourth move, Czentovic thought again for an endless time, did he lose his composure, and he suddenly hissed at him, "Just play already!"

Czentovic looked up coolly. "To my knowledge, we agreed on ten minutes per move. I don't play with shorter time limits."

Dr. B. bit his lip; I noticed how, under the table, his sole was rocking impatiently and more and more restlessly against the floor, and I became increasingly nervous myself by the oppressive premonition that something terrible was rising within him. In fact, a second incident occurred on the eighth move. Dr. B., who had waited more and more uncontrollably, couldn't hold back his tension any longer; he moved back and forth and began to drum unconsciously with his fingers on the table.

Once again, Czentovic lifted his heavy, peasant-like head. "May I ask you not to drum. It disturbs me. I can't play like this."

"Ha!" laughed Dr. B. shortly. "That's evident."

Czentovic's forehead turned red. "What do you mean?" he asked sharply and angrily.

Dr. B. laughed again briefly and maliciously. "Nothing. Just that you are obviously very nervous."

Czentovic remained silent and lowered his head. Only after seven minutes did he make the next move, and the game dragged on at this deadly pace. Czentovic seemed to stiffen more and more; finally, he used the maximum agreed-upon thinking time before making every move, and from one interval to another, our friend's behavior became stranger. It seemed as if he no longer took any interest in the game but was preoccupied with something completely different. He stopped his feverish pacing and sat motionless in his place. Staring into the void with a fixed and almost maniacal gaze, he murmured unintelligible words continuously; either he got lost in endless combinations, or he was working—this was my deepest suspicion—on completely different games because each time Czentovic finally moved, he had to be brought back from his absent-mindedness. Then he always needed a few minutes to get back into the situation. More and more, I suspected that he had actually forgotten Czentovic and all of us in this cold form of madness, which could suddenly discharge in some violence. And indeed, at the nineteenth move, the crisis broke out. Hardly had Czentovic moved his piece when Dr. B. suddenly, without looking at the board, advanced his bishop three squares and shouted so loudly that we all jumped.

"Check! Check to the king!"

Expecting a special move, we immediately looked at the board. But after a minute, what none of us expected happened. Czentovic slowly raised his head, looking—for the first time—in our circle from one to the other. He seemed to be enjoying himself immeasurably because gradually a satisfied and distinctly mocking smile began to appear on his lips.

Only after savoring this triumph, still incomprehensible to us, to the fullest, did he turn with false politeness to our group.

"Sorry - but I see no check. Do any of the gentlemen see a check against my king, perhaps?"

We looked at the board and then anxiously at Dr. B. Czentovic's king square was indeed—any child could see it—completely covered by a pawn against the bishop, so no check was possible. We became uneasy. Could our friend, in his fervor, have pushed a piece too far or too close?

Prompted by our silence, Dr. B. also stared at the board and began to stammer anxiously, "But the king belongs on h1... it's placed wrong, completely wrong. You've moved incorrectly! Everything is completely wrong on this board... the pawn belongs on g5, not g4... This is an entirely different game... This is..." He suddenly stopped. I had grabbed him forcefully by the arm, or rather, pinched his arm so hard that even in his feverish confusion, he must have felt my grip. He turned around and stared at me like a sleepwalker.

"What...what do you want?" I said nothing but "Remember!" while simultaneously running my finger over the scar on his hand. He involuntarily followed my movement, his eye staring blankly at the blood-red line. Then, he suddenly started to tremble, and a shudder ran through his entire body. "For God's sake," he whispered with pale lips. "Did I say or do something nonsensical... am I, in the end, again...?"

Chess

"No," I whispered softly. "But you must immediately stop the game; it is high time. Remember what the doctor told you!"

Dr. B. stood up abruptly. "I apologize for my foolish mistake," he said in his old polite voice, bowing to Czentovic. "It is, of course, pure nonsense what I said. Naturally, it remains your game."

Then, he turned to us. "I must also apologize to the gentlemen. But I warned you in advance; you should not expect too much from me. Forgive the disgrace—it was the last time I attempted to play chess." He bowed and left, in the same humble and mysterious manner in which he had first appeared. Only I knew why this man would never touch a chessboard again, while the others were left a bit confused, with the uncertain feeling of narrowly escaping something uncomfortable and dangerous. "Damned fool!" grumbled McConnor in his disappointment. Czentovic, at last, rose from his seat and cast one more glance at the half-finished game. "Too bad," he said generously. "The attack was not so badly arranged. For an amateur, this gentleman is unusually talented."

Stefan Zweig preparing *Schachnovelle*

ABOUT THE SERIES

Decatur Dixon of Shelby, North Carolina is widely read and widely travelled. While he has sampled every dish and libation placed in front of him and fishes at least once a week, his favorite activity is reading. Every genre, every era. This book is the fifth in a curated series of favorites. Decatur Dixon Publishing specializes in illustrated classics as well as poetry, philosophy, and writing that sits between genres of all stripes.

Lula Crowder is a bohemian of the highest order. Classically trained, she has offered curated shows as well as her own work in the salons of New York, San Francisco, Savannah, and elsewhere. Her book illustrations are best known for appearing in manilla envelopes tucked into library editions and borrowed collections as gifts to future readers. Inspired by artists as diverse as Wanda Gag, Ray Johnson, Mika Rotenberg, Lebbeus Woods, and Mike Kelley, her drawings always add a fresh and at times winningly critical dimension.

We hope you will enjoy other books in this series

The Sword of Wood: an illustrated version of a little-known tale.
By G.K. Chesterton. Illustrations by Lula Crowder

Pierre and Jean: an illustrated classic, with bonus essay "The Novel"
By Guy de Maupassant. Illustrations by Lula Crowder

The Light Princess: an illustrated novella.
By George Macdonald. Illustrations by Lula Crowder.

R.U.R. (Rossum's Universal Robots): A Fantastic Melodrama in Three Acts and an Epilogue.
By Karel Čapek. Illustrations by Lula Crowder.

Printed in Great Britain
by Amazon